To my niece, Chelsea,
a shining star in my universe.
—T.C.

For her royal flatness, Yuna.
—S.S.

Quill Tree Books is an imprint of HarperCollins Publishers.

Zuri Ray and the Backyard Bash
Copyright © 2022 by HarperCollins Publishers
All rights reserved. Manufactured in Italy.
No part of this book may be used or reproduced in any manner whatsoever
without written permission except in the case of brief quotations embodied in critical
articles and reviews. For information address HarperCollins Children's Books,
a division of HarperCollins Publishers, 195 Broadway, New York, NY 10007.
www.harpercollinschildrens.com

Library of Congress Control Number: 2021942561
ISBN 978-0-06-291804-8

The artist used Adobe Photoshop to create the digital illustrations for this book.
Typography by Rachel Zegar
22 23 24 25 26   RTLO   10 9 8 7 6 5 4 3 2 1
❖
First Edition

ZURI RAY

and the
Backyard Bash

Written by Tami Charles

Illustrated by Sharon Sordo

Quill Tree Books
An Imprint of HarperCollinsPublishers

Zuri Ray loved a good party.
The food . . . the friends . . .
and, of course, the FUN!

"We should have an end-of-summer bash!" Zuri suggested to her parents, who happily agreed.

Zuri was thrilled . . . until the planning began.

"Let's play '80s music!" Mom said. "I'll try that olive Jell-O mold recipe!"

"And let's reuse those cute decorations from Zuri's third birthday party," Dad added.

"Mom and Dad are joking, right?" Zuri's
sister, Remi, asked.
But Zuri knew better.
This was a party-planning *emergency*!

Mom couldn't help but overhear. "You don't like our ideas?" she asked.

"They sound like a disaster!" Zuri complained.

Dad chuckled. "How about *you* take the lead then?"

"I thought you'd never ask. Remi, Sherlock Hound, round up the troops!"

Minutes later, Zuri and Remi's friends gathered in their backyard.

There was Lupe from school, Joseph and Tessa from church, the Patel twins from swim class, and Jessie, Zuri's BFFD—that's best friend from diapers, in case you didn't know.

"We have party problems, people! Our first order of business is food," Zuri said. "There shall be no olives and no Jell-O, especially combined."

Everyone giggled.

Lupe called out, "My abuela can make tacos and desserts!"

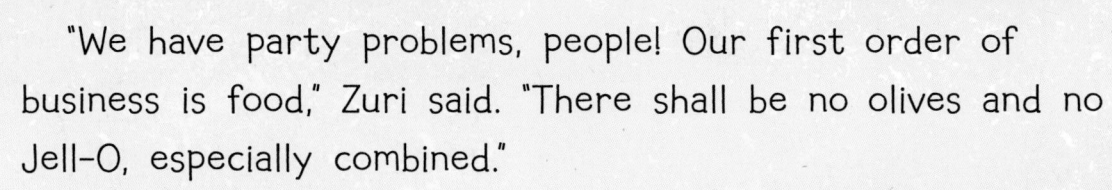

"My dad does the best barbecue!" Joseph added.

"Perfect!" Zuri checked food off her to-do list.

"What about the yard?" Zuri asked.
"It needs some pizzazz."
"My uncle taught me how to make
paper roses!" Tessa said.

"Our stepmom has holiday lights!" the Patel twins added, then squealed, "Jinx!"

The backyard would go from drab to fab in no time! Zuri checked decorations off her list.

"And, finally, we'll need entertainment!" Zuri said.
Playing old-school music was a big no-no! But what could give the party some oomph?
"Satya and I can do magic tricks," Nanda Patel offered.

"Ooh, dancing!" Remi, Lupe, and Tessa peeped.

"Country singer here!" Joseph exclaimed.

These were the most splendid ideas.
"Let's make it a talent show!" Zuri exclaimed.
Of course, Zuri would create the most perfect
performance. And so would her friends!
It would be the most extraordinary, anything-but-
ordinary backyard bash ever!

Zuri and her friends spent the week preparing.

Zuri practiced her top secret grand finale that would knock everyone's socks off!

Finally, the big day arrived.
The yard looked dazzling.
The scent of delicious foods swirled in the air.
Friends and families gathered to eat and share.

Soon it was time for lights, excitement, action!
Zuri felt butterflies in her stomach.

"What if the audience doesn't clap?" Zuri whispered.
And then she worried some more. What if the microphone
stopped working? What if it rained?

Dad grabbed Zuri's hand: "It doesn't have to be perfect.
It just has to be fun."

Fun, shmun! Nothing would stand in the way of Zuri's
perfect show.

First, Lupe danced to music
from *Swan Lake*.
Graceful grand jetés!
Sweeping pirouettes!

But halfway through the
performance, Lupe forgot
her moves.
Oh no!

Jessie looked at a worried Zuri.
"Do you remember what we
learned in ballet?"
Zuri gulped. They had taken
ballet at camp earlier that
summer.
Jessie was a pro. Zuri? Well, she
tried her best.
"Follow me!" Jessie said.

Jessie did a plié, then a fouetté, like a prima ballerina.
Lupe and Zuri did the same.
The audience cheered.

The girls curtsied.
Whew! That was close!
"Thanks for having my back, girls," Lupe said.
"That's what friends are for." Zuri smiled.

Next, the Patel twins made things disappear
like magic, and Joseph yodeled a country tune . . .

and Remi and Tessa hip-hopped like nobody's business!

Finally, it was time for Zuri's grand finale.
From the very first note, the crowd went wild!
Until a squirrel zipped across the stage, holding . . .

Was that a toy?
A bone?
A toy bone?
Sherlock Hound couldn't resist finding out.
His friends wanted to help too.

Zuri stopped singing.
Then she panicked. "Sherlock, noooo!"

Zuri chased

and stumbled

and tumbled

and then . . .

CRASH!

Zuri's perfect, extraordinary, anything-but-ordinary performance was ruined!

"What a nightmare!" Zuri sobbed to her mom. "Can everyone please just go home?"

"Sometimes things don't go as planned. It's okay to try something new and unexpected. But whatever you do, just have fun," Mom said.

Mom held Zuri close. Zuri could feel her mom's warm heart. She could hear her guests chanting.

"Zuri! Zuri! Zuri!"

Then Zuri remembered why she wanted to throw this party in the first place.

The FUN!

Zuri picked up her guitar again and marched onstage.
She strummed a chord and began to sing.

This time louder and prouder, until the whole audience rocked, rattled, and ROLLED!

"Bravo! Hooray!"

Zuri took the biggest, most dramatic bow.

Zuri beamed at her friends, the best party planners in town!
The backyard bash wasn't a complete catastrophe. Especially
since Zuri knew the perfect way to end the show . . .

"Who wants dessert?"

And there was nothing more FUN than that.